READING CORNER

PHONICS

Miss Drew at the Zoo

Written by
Sue Graves

Illustrated by
Tim Archbold

Practising long vowel phonemes,
CVCC and CCVC plus polysyllabic words

First published in 2010 by
Franklin Watts
338 Euston Road
London NW1 3BH

Franklin Watts Australia
Hachette Children's Books
Level 17/207 Kent Street
Sydney NSW 2000

Text © Sue Graves 2010
Illustration © Tim Archbold 2010

A CIP catalogue record for this book is available from the British Library.

ISBN: 978 0 7496 9169 1 (hbk)
ISBN: 978 0 7496 9178 3 (pbk)

Series Editor: Jackie Hamley
Series Advisors: Dr Barrie Wade,
 Dr Hilary Minns
Series Designer: Jonathan Hair

Printed in China

Franklin Watts is a division of Hachette Children's Books, an Hachette UK company www.hachette.co.uk

There is a puzzle at the end of this book.
Here are the answers for you to check later!

The matching words are:
zoo flew, new, too
Troy boy, joy, toy
snake brake, flake, take
green bean, lean, teen

The children were at the
zoo with Miss Drew.

"Look, Miss Drew!" cried Troy.

"A monkey's got out."

"Don't be annoying, Troy!"
said Miss Drew.

First they went to see

the elephants.

The monkey took
Miss Drew's green hat.

"The monkey's got your hat,
Miss Drew," cried Troy.

"Don't be annoying, Troy!"

said Miss Drew.

Then they went to see the snakes.

13

The monkey took
Miss Drew's drink.

"Now the monkey's got your drink, Miss Drew," cried Troy.

"Don't be annoying, Troy!"

said Miss Drew.

Next they went to see the big cats.

Lions

This time *all* the children
saw the monkey.

They saw it take Miss Drew's lunchbox.

They saw it take out
her sandwich.

"Time for our snacks," said Miss Drew. "But where's my lunchbox? Where's my drink? And where's my hat?"

"The monkey took them!"
all the children cried. "Look!"

"Oh, that is so annoying!"
said Miss Drew.

And all the children laughed!

Puzzle Time!

Match the words that rhyme
to the pictures.

zoo

boy

bean

flake

flew

Troy

teen

take

snake

too

lean

joy

toy

green

new

brake

See page 2 for answers.

Notes for parents and teachers

READING CORNER PHONICS has been structured to provide maximum support for children learning to read through synthetic phonics. The stories are designed for independent reading but may also be used by adults for sharing with young children.

The teaching of early reading through synthetic phonics focuses on the 44 sounds in the English language, and how these sounds correspond to their written form in the 26 letters of the alphabet. Carefully controlled vocabulary makes these books accessible for children at different stages of phonics teaching, progressing from simple CVC (consonant-vowel-consonant) words such as "top" (t-o-p) to trisyllabic words such as "messenger" (mess-en-ger). READING CORNER PHONICS allows children to read words in context, and also provides visual clues and repetition to further support their reading. These books will help develop the all important confidence in the new reader, and encourage a love of reading that will last a lifetime!

If you are reading this book with a child, here are a few tips:

1. Talk about the story before you start reading. Look at the cover and the title. What might the story be about? Why might the child like it?

2. Encourage the child to reread the story, and to retell the story in their own words, using the illustrations to remind them what has happened.

3. Discuss the story and see if the child can relate it to their own experience, or perhaps compare it to another story they know.

4. Give praise! Small mistakes need not always be corrected. If a child is stuck on a word, ask them to try and sound it out and then blend it together again, or model this yourself. For example "wish" w-i-sh "wish".

READING CORNER PHONICS covers two grades of synthetic phonics teaching, with three levels at each grade. Each level has a certain number of words per story, indicated by the number of bars on the spine of the book:

GRADE 1

	50 words	CVC words with short vowel sounds
	70 words	CVC words plus sounds of more than one letter
	100 words	Sounds of more than one letter, simple polysyllabic words

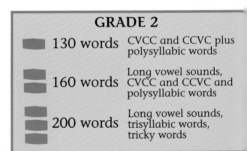

GRADE 2

	130 words	CVCC and CCVC plus polysyllabic words
	160 words	Long vowel sounds, CVCC and CCVC and polysyllabic words
	200 words	Long vowel sounds, trisyllabic words, tricky words